The Extraordinary Adventures
of Ordinary Basil

The Extraordinary Adventures of Ordinary Basil

by WILEY MILLER

THE BLUE SKY PRESS · AN IMPRINT OF SCHOLASTIC INC. · NEW YORK

THE BLUE SKY PRESS

Text copyright © 2006 by Wiley Miller
Illustrations copyright © 2006 by Wiley Miller
All rights reserved.

Special thanks to Bonnie Verburg for helping Basil find direction,
to Robert Martin Staenberg for lending his invaluable perspective,
and to Ira Ingber for his extraordinary hard work, dedication,
and most important, belief.

Library of Congress catalog card number available.

ISBN [HC]: 0-439-85665-5 / [BF]: 0-439-90178-2

10 9 8 7 6 5 4 3 2 1   06 07 08 09 10

Printed in Singapore   46

First printing, November 2006

Book design by Kathleen Westray

For every kid who thinks they're ordinary.

CHAPTER ONE
Ordinary Basil

IT WAS SNOWING. Again. It always seemed to be snowing on the coast of Maine in January. Being shut in was Basil Pepperell's lot, and he accepted it, just as he accepted everything else in his ordinary life.

"Most children would give anything to live in a lighthouse, darling," Basil's mother told him as he sat slumped at his bedroom window, watching the snow pile higher. It was little comfort for a 12-year-old boy longing for adventure.

"That's because they don't live in one," Basil muttered. "They have no idea just how ordinary it really is here. Nothing exciting ever happens."

"Well, what's wrong with ordinary?" Mrs. Pepperell shot back in frustration. "If you only had

extraordinary events in your life, then nothing would seem special anymore. The ordinary things are what make the special moments worth savoring!"

Basil turned away from the window and looked at his mother.

"Think about it," she said as she headed to the door. "You can either sit and mope about how boring your life is, or you can make the most of what life hands you. Things can change. It's your choice."

Basil did think about it, and he had to admit there was truth in her words.

But change meant that he had to do something. He had to go to an adventure, not wait for an adventure to come to him.

As Basil sat at his window, a tune began to play in his mind. It was a melody he couldn't remember hearing before, yet it was somehow familiar. He began to whistle the tune, first quietly, then louder. Whistling was one of Basil's talents, but he never really cared for it. "Where is being a good whistler ever going to get me?" he said aloud with a sigh.

A voice unexpectedly wafted through the window. "Farther than you might imagine, dear boy!"

Living in a lighthouse, Basil was used to the occasional fisherman passing by and stopping for some conversation. He looked down to see which fisherman it was, but no one was there. Then he heard the voice again.

"No, dear boy . . . up here!"

Leaning out as far as he could, Basil turned and looked up. He stood motionless at his bedroom window, which was three stories above the rocks and sea below. His jaw dropped, and his eyes bulged. He blinked in disbelief.

Basil found himself staring directly at the bottom of a boat!

As this impossible sight began to slowly and silently glide down, Basil backed away.

Soon the amazing ship reached the level of Basil's window. He saw that the boat was suspended in air by an enormous balloon. A jovial man at the helm sported a tall top hat and epaulets on his double-breasted coat, indicating some sort of military rank. But it was unlike any military uniform Basil had ever seen.

The gentleman was grinning broadly. His face was almost obscured by a robust mustache that nearly reached the width of his shoulders. "Sorry to interrupt, but could you be so kind as to direct me to the town of York?" the stranger asked in a soothing and friendly baritone voice. Basil oddly felt at ease.

Is this real? Basil wondered. It was 1899, when air travel was still a dream. But when he felt the cold wind blowing on his face, Basil knew he wasn't dreaming. His eyes opened wider. Suddenly his bewilderment was replaced by an exciting notion. Could this possibly be a great opportunity? "Finally," he whispered under a growing smile, "something interesting is happening to me!"

"Can you point me in the right direction?" the strange man asked, still grinning.

Basil knew such opportunities don't come around often, and when they do, they don't linger very long. If he was going to make the most of it, he would have to act now.

"Perhaps," he
said nervously, "I should
come along and show you the way, sir."

The man let out a bellowing laugh so loud it shook
the house. "Ah," he said with a twinkle in his eyes. "A
lad seeking adventure, eh? Jolly good! Hop aboard,
young man, and begin your adventure!"

Stepping up to the ledge of his window, Basil
prepared to leap. Suddenly, the airship that looked so
close before now seemed far away. *This is the first step*,
he told himself. *It's now or never. . . .*

With that, Basil made the mightiest leap of his life.

He quickly realized that he didn't have anything to
fear, for his right leg easily cleared the ship's railing.
But it wasn't the leap he needed to worry about. It was

the landing. As his left foot trailed behind, it clipped the edge of the rail. Basil was thrown off balance, and he plunged awkwardly into a neatly coiled pile of rope.

Despite Basil's crash landing, the kind old man didn't laugh. Instead he helped Basil to his feet, knowing the boy was embarrassed.

"Welcome aboard, Laddy," he said. "We pilots know how difficult it is to make any leap at all."

As the great airship slowly rose above the lighthouse, Basil peered over the edge of the stern. His home looked quite different from this angle, making him pause. As they sailed off, Basil felt an unexpected pang. He had never been away from his family before, and he hadn't even said good-bye. He wasn't sure if he was scared or excited . . . or both. Soon the thrill of the unknown overshadowed his fear. "My wish came true," he said out loud. "I'm going on an adventure!"

"That's the spirit!" the old man said with a grin. "I heard your whistle, you know. It's an unusual lad who knows *that* song."

Before Basil could ask any questions, the gentleman continued. "But I should warn you of the ancient curse, dear boy . . . be careful what you wish for—you just might get it."

Basil smiled even more. *Danger!* he thought to himself. *How extraordinary!*

"I believe introductions are in order," said the gentleman as he steered the preposterous airship higher and higher into the clouds. "My name is Professor Angus McGookin."

His deep, musical voice had a gurgling resonance, as if it came from the very depths of the sea. But at the same time, it was as soothing as the surface breeze. "And what might your name be, Lad?"

"It might be something interesting," the boy solemnly replied. "But it isn't. My name is just Basil. My life is so ordinary. I wasn't named for a hero. I was named after a common herb."

"Ordinary, eh?" the professor said while turning the great wheel and pulling some levers. "Let's see what we can do about that." And he began to hum that same mysterious tune that Basil had been whistling when the airship first came into sight.

Basil looked down and gasped as he saw that they were over the Isle of Shoals. In just minutes, they had traveled miles and miles—what would have taken hours of sailing. As the ship rose higher and higher, the islands seemed to grow smaller and smaller. Now Basil could see the entire southern Maine coastline, all the way up to Portland. And now they were almost higher than birds could fly. And as he stood mesmerized, Basil remembered why he was invited aboard in the first place. He was supposed to help the professor with directions.

"The town of York is right down there, Professor," Basil reported, pointing to a place just inland from the York harbor.

"Thank you, dear boy," the professor said without looking at the place where Basil was pointing. "We'll get to that later. There's something I think you might want to see first."

The professor pulled on levers and turned dials that were carved into panels beside the great steering

wheel of the ship. They were all quite complex. As
Basil tried to make sense of the dials, the ship went
into a steep climb up to the clouds. He felt himself
sliding back toward the stern. He held on for dear life.
Soon, they were encased in the thick white fog of a
cloud, and Basil could barely see his hand in front of
his face. As they continued to rise, the cloud became
thinner, and the sun began to shine through.

This delicious warmth was a pleasant departure from the dreary grey skies and endless winter snow below. Basil closed his eyes and tilted his face to soak up the glowing rays of the sun. Then he sensed a flash of brilliant light. When he opened his eyes, he was blinded for a moment. Then, his eyes began to adjust to the light. There was something out there! What was it? He couldn't tell.

Gradually, the spots in front of his eyes began to fade, and he was able to focus again. Basil's hands slowly dropped to his side as he stared up into the heavens in stunned disbelief. As the clouds parted, what he saw could not be real.

A city! A towering, glimmering city floated on the clouds. Each incredible building was connected to another with a complex system of glass tubes.

Finally, remembering to breathe, Basil managed to force out one word. "Extraordinary . . ."

As if the sight of a floating city wasn't enough, Basil noticed strange objects swirling around outside the city domes. When the objects came closer, Basil saw what they were—ships, coming and going. They were ships like the professor's—only some of them were much bigger.

Circling around the ships were still other things, smaller and faster. At first Basil thought they must be birds, but they were much too big to be birds—at least any birds he had ever seen. They soared on majestically huge wings. And on each of their backs, a person was guiding them!

These strange, bird-like creatures reminded him of stories he'd heard from English sailors. The stories were about recent scientific discoveries of huge bones that belonged to gigantic, ancient beasts. They were called "dinosaurs." Could these giant, flying birds be some kind of dinosaur?

Basil's mind was reeling. He felt his knees buckle as every sense in his body went into shock.

"Steady, Laddie,"
the jovial professor
said as he began to tie
the ship to the dock. "The air is
a bit thin here. You'll feel better once we get inside."

In his dizzy state, Basil wondered if he was
dreaming. But the dream was so real! And just when
he thought it couldn't get any more fantastic, they
walked through the portal and entered a gleaming
tower. With a knowing look, the professor simply
smiled. "Welcome to Helios!" he said.

Still trying to catch his breath, Basil was only able to sputter a few words. "Bu-bu-but how? This isn't p-p-possible. . . ."

"Wherever there is life, dear boy," the professor assured him, "there are endless possibilities. Our only limitations are those of our imaginations."

"How many people know about this place, sir?" Basil asked as he began to regain his wits.

"To date," the professor replied with understated glee, "the sum total of Earth-dwellers who know about Helios is . . . one. And guess who that one is?"

Suddenly Basil didn't feel so ordinary anymore.

Taking in the astonishing view inside the circular tower where he stood, Basil inhaled deeply. The air was thicker so he could now think more clearly. The tower was filled with soft music—wonderful music. It made Basil feel curiously happy inside. As he peered down over a railing, Basil could see that this tower had many levels, bustling with activity.

On the level above, a rail car transported people to other towers in the city. It moved much faster than any locomotive back in Maine, and it traveled without any sound. Then Basil heard a whooshing noise, as if steam were escaping. There, flying in the open air, a man in a balloon-like suit zoomed by, powered by cylinders attached to his belt.

"What's that?" Basil shouted excitedly, pointing at the man as he zipped past.

"That's a man in a helium suit—one of our latest developments!" the professor replied.

Walking over to one of the glass connecting tubes, Basil took in a view of the entire city. "How is this possible?" he asked in wonder.

"That, dear boy," the professor replied, "is a secret that has been closely guarded for hundreds and hundreds of years."

"Well, where did it come from? How long has it been here? How could such a fantastic place exist without anyone knowing about it?"

"Ah," the professor said with a laugh, "just the inquisitive mind I was hoping for!"

Angus McGookin then heaved a gentle sigh. He seemed to be gathering his thoughts about where to begin his long and complicated story.

As they strolled the corridors of the amazing city, the professor began his history lesson. Basil was eager to take it all in.

"Long, long ago," the professor began in a matter-of-fact manner, "when people still believed the world was flat, Helios was a civilization that flourished in science, music, engineering, art, and philosophy." He paused and saw that Basil was hanging on every

word. "Have you ever noticed, in school, how history
is taught as eras of warfare? That your history lessons
are divided up by when a war began and ended?" the
professor asked.

Basil pondered the question, mentally skimming through the history lessons he had been taught in school—the Revolutionary War, the Civil War, the Crimean War—on and on. "You're right, sir," Basil replied, feeling a little ashamed of his schooling. "I never noticed that before."

"Well, the history of Helios," the professor continued, "is the history of human accomplishment, not human self-destruction. Our history is about great discoveries, not about wars."

"Then why doesn't everyone know about Helios?" Basil asked.

"Excellent question," the professor said.

"To the rest of the world, Helios has been steeped in myth and legend. Throughout the ages, it has been written off as the delusions of sailors who got lost at sea."

Basil was fascinated. *Sailors . . . ?* he wondered. Back in Maine, he'd heard a lot of tales about life out at sea. Fishermen told stories that had been passed down from generation to generation about an ancient land that was somehow hidden in the Atlantic Ocean. It was fabled that this mysterious place had been the birthplace of Greek philosophy and the engineering that built the Egyptian pyramids. Could it be that they weren't fables after all?

"Umm-mm," Basil stammered. "Was it always called Helios, sir?"

"No," the professor said with an approving smile. "You're putting things together pretty quickly, aren't you? It has been known by dozens of names throughout time. Those who stumbled onto our shores called it Eden, Valhalla, and many other names. But the one that seemed to stick in mythology was . . ."

". . . Atlantis!" Basil
said, finishing the
professor's sentence with
breathless excitement.

"Yes, Atlantis was
one of the more popular
names. But we call it
Helios. It's a place above
others, a remarkably
advanced civilization.
And now that earthly
wars have threatened
to destroy our planet,
Helios is literally in
the sky. Dear boy," the
professor continued,
"it's taken all of our
technology to find
a place to keep our
civilization safe. And
that place, right now,
is up here in the clouds."

CHAPTER TWO

Helios

AS BASIL accompanied Angus McGookin down another corridor, the professor once again began to hum the oddly familiar tune that had drawn him to Basil in the first place. Then he opened an enormous door and led Basil into a great rotunda library.

The professor opened volume after volume of encyclopedia-sized books. Basil learned that every great leap forward in art, music, and science around the world were gifts of knowledge from the people of Helios. The Dark Ages that plagued Europe came to an end when the people of Helios inspired the Renaissance. Later, they helped create the Industrial Revolution.

"But," the professor said with a sigh of despair, "the peace brought by Helios never lasted. People always had a primitive urge for power that led them to war, and every war ended our attempt to teach them art and science—and the importance of peace."

"Is that why Helios was kept hidden from the rest of the world?" Basil asked, now feeling more ordinary than ever, and very embarassed by his ancestry.

"I'm afraid so, dear boy," the professor replied. "As men took to sailing the open seas, occasionally some would get caught in a storm and were blown to our shores. When we repaired their ships and helped them find their way home, they talked about their adventure. At first they weren't believed, and their stories were dismissed as tall tales. But we knew it was only a matter of time before more people came to Helios, and with them, warfare. So our scientists went to work on taking us where we couldn't be reached . . . the clouds."

"But how was this done?" Basil asked. "How can an entire city float on clouds?"

The professor smiled. "That's a secret only fully known by three of our people at a time. This assures

the safety and security of Helios. But only those
on the High Council know who the three people are.
And should something happen to those three, the
knowledge would be lost forever."

"Do you know who the three people are?" Basil
asked impetuously.

The professor just gave him that same smile again,
only this time he didn't answer.

Pulling out his pocket watch, the professor gave a start. "My goodness!" he bellowed. "Look at the time! We need to get you home, Laddie. I know the High Council will be most pleased to know you've finally been found. But it's time to go. Wait here while I get the airship ready." Then he bounded out with surprising agility for such a rotund man of his age.

Going home? Basil didn't want to hear that yet. *Finally found? The High Council?* Basil didn't even know why he'd been allowed to come to Helios in the first place. But he was even more surprised to hear what came next.

"You're so lucky. . . ."

Following the sound of a soft voice, Basil turned to
see a girl spying from the shadows of a doorway.

"Lucky?" Basil asked incredulously. "Me?"

"Yes, you," the girl responded as her shyness gave
way to a sudden boldness. "*You* get to live on the
ground."

Her words left Basil speechless. But they paled in
comparison to what she said next.

"It's just so . . . so ordinary here."

"Ordinary?" Basil heard himself blurt out. "You think your life here is ordinary?"

"Yes!" the girl exclaimed. "I've been here all my life and know every square inch of this city. I'm forbidden to leave it. I want to see the world. I don't care how dangerous they tell me it is down there. I want some adventure—just like you have every day on the ground!"

Basil was dumbstruck. How could anyone find life in such an extraordinary place as Helios ordinary? This girl certainly didn't know much about life in coastal Maine. How it snowed all the time. And how day followed ordinary day. And here she was, living in the most incredibly fascinating place in the universe. . . .

Seeing that Basil seemed completely flustered, the girl changed the subject. "I'm sorry. How rude of me to not introduce myself first. My name is Louise."

"Uh . . . hello, Louise. M-m-my name is Basil," he stammered. "Do-do you really think that my life on the ground is more interesting than yours up here?"

"Absolutely," Louise said, brightening up. "I'd trade places with you in a minute!"

"What an intriguing idea," Basil thought aloud. It occurred to him that this might be the start of a very long and strange friendship.

"Professor McGookin will be back soon to take you home," Louise said with a sad sigh. "I wish I could go with you." Basil was about to reply, but he stopped short when a man zipped past the window in a helium suit. Mistaking Basil's amazed silence for  stubborn resistance, Louise tried harder to persuade him. "Please! I'll let you take a ride on Beatrice if you let me go back to the ground with you!"

"Umm-mm," Basil stammered. "What . . . who . . . is Beatrice?"

"My pteranodon, of course." Louise found everything about Basil surprising. "Don't people on the ground have pteranodons, too?"

Letting out an exasperated sigh, Basil muttered under his breath, "She thinks her life is ordinary?"

The giant creature named Beatrice looked frightening, but it was obviously tame in the hands of Louise.

Well . . . Louise has probably handled a pteranodon all her life, Basil told himself, steeling his nerves as Louise coaxed him onto the back of her pet. When they took flight and soared away from the towers, Basil inhaled deeply. *What's the worst that could happen?* he asked himself.

That question was going to be answered very soon.

As Basil and Louise flew up above the shield of clouds and into clear blue skies, they could see everything below. You might think that someone on the ground would spot them, but Louise wasn't concerned. She knew perfectly well that Beatrice couldn't be seen with the naked eye from below. In order to see her pteranodon, someone would need to be intentionally looking for them through a telescope. The odds of that were remote.

Unfortunately, today she was wrong. They were indeed being watched.

"At last . . ." came a thick Germanic accent from behind an extremely powerful telescope. The man had been scanning the edges of the clouds since dawn. "I haf finally located Helios! I must haf zair power!"

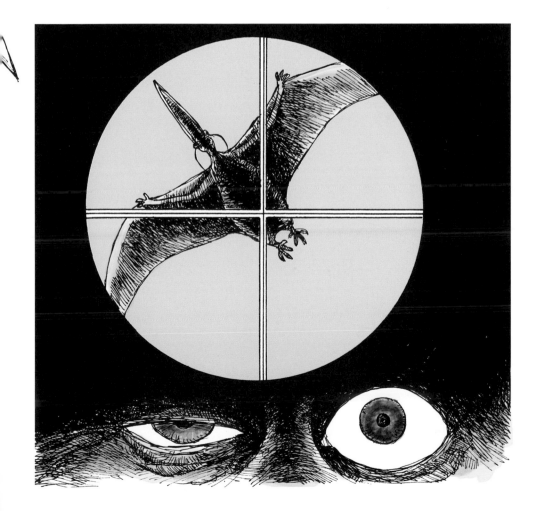

With his spirits soaring as high as the great flying reptile, Basil noticed a strange, unfamiliar sensation. He was happy! No, it was more than happiness—he was positively thrilled!

"I never want this to end," he whispered to himself. "Please let this go on forever!"

But like most things in life, it *would* end. And it would end a lot sooner than Basil and Louise expected.

As Louise steered Beatrice to bank into a glide of thermals, she glimpsed a flash of light on the ground. She quickly turned to Basil, snapping him out of his rare burst of happiness with an urgent order.

"Hold on tight!"

Before Basil could even think to ask why, Louise leaned back and pulled on the reins with all her might. "Pull up, Bea!" she shouted. "Pull up!"

The mighty pteranodon jerked back, halting their forward glide. At that very second, a harpoon—one like whalers used—whistled by in front of them. Luckily, it quickly lost energy and fell harmlessly away.

Louise's sharp wits and quick reflexes had allowed them to narrowly avert disaster. Still shaken by the attack, Louise regained control of level flight. Then she steered Beatrice back toward the safety of the clouds.

But something felt
wrong. "Beatrice?"
Louise called out.
Her powerful
pteranodon was
suddenly flying
faster than
before. Could
Beatrice be
. . . lighter?
    "Basil . . .?"
Louise shouted
above the sound
of rushing wind. But
there was no answer. With grim
determination, Louise leaned
into Beatrice and said with
loving urgency,
"Dive, Bea . . .
FETCH!"

Meanwhile, having lost his grip in the unexpected jolt of a harpoon attack, Basil was plummeting to Earth. Mercifully, the rapid approach of the ground caused a quick blackout. *Wham!* Basil closed his eyes. Immediately everything vanished.

History will never record Basil Pepperell's accomplishment of being the first skydiver, even though he was completely unconscious as it happened. While he plunged toward the ground, Louise was sending Beatrice into a steep dive. Luckily, the powerful flying reptile quickly caught up with Basil. Beatrice knew exactly what to do from there. She spread her enormous talons as if she were capturing prey, only this time she grabbed gently.

Seconds before Basil was to hit the ocean, Beatrice carefully snared him. "Gotcha!" Louise shouted in victory. But it was to be short-lived.

Watching the dramatic rescue from behind a telescope was a tall man—a very tall man. He had long limbs that moved with the awkward grace of a stork, and he had a nose to match. His thin, black hair was slicked back with oily efficiency, and his thick eyebrows encircled beady red eyes. Turning to face his hideous, hunched assistant, the tall man said with malevolent calm, "Reload za harpoon. It appears ve haf anozer chance. . . ."

With Basil now safe in her grip, Beatrice flapped her mighty wings to gain altitude and return to the clouds. But with Basil hanging below instead of riding on her back, Beatrice was forced to fly slowly.

Kaboom! The muffled sound of a cannon shot echoed from below.

"Faster, Bea!" Louise shouted. "Faster!"

Another harpoon whizzed past them, arching over Beatrice's head. But there was something different about this new harpoon. Unlike the first one, this one had a second line attached.

"It's not a line!" Louise shouted to Beatrice. "It's a snare!"

Looping around Beatrice's
head, the snare tightened when
the harpoon fell back to Earth. With
the other end of the line firmly anchored
below, the rope abruptly jerked Beatrice backward.

"Bull's-eye!" the tall man shouted with evil glee.

The violent yank on her neck made Beatrice lose her grip. Louise could only watch helplessly as Basil dropped, unconscious, into the dark waters of the bay.

"I have to save Basil!" Louise cried.

But first, she had to save herself.

Splash! When Basil hit the cold water of the dark bay, he was jolted back to consciousness. *Where am I? How did I get here?* Deep in the icy water, Basil didn't know which way was up, or which way was down. All he knew was this: he couldn't breathe!

He was dazed and disoriented, but his survival instincts immediately took over. Because he grew up by the ocean, he knew how to swim—and luckily he could swim well.

Underwater, Basil followed what little light he could see. When he broke the surface, he tried to fill his empty lungs as fast as he could. His teeth chattered from the cold.

Slowly he began to make his way to the shore. He was struggling to haul himself up on the rocks when he noticed an old house nearby. He was soaked to the bone and shivering so badly he could barely walk—but walk he must, and as fast as he could for the shelter of the house. Louise and Beatrice were nowhere in sight. No doubt they were off looking for him.

Deep woods had hidden most of the house, and when he was closer he saw that the house wasn't just big—it was HUGE. Smoke coming out of the chimneys made Basil think there must be someone home to help him. Oddly, the chimneys did not give the house a warm and friendly appearance. In fact, they belched thick, black clouds as if they were factory smokestacks.

Getting closer still, Basil could see a strange mechanical object on the very top of the house. At first, he couldn't quite make it out. Then, with a chill, he knew what it was—a harpoon cannon like those he had seen on whaling schooners. In it was the same kind of harpoon that had been shot at Beatrice! But why?

Frightened, he approached the house with caution. Cold and wet as he was, he would take a look around the building before knocking on the door.

A tall iron fence topped with sharp spikes surrounded the house, and guard towers overlooked the grounds. Basil was able to squeeze through the fence undetected, as it wasn't designed to thwart a

12-year-old boy so slight of frame. Still shivering, he silently began to circle the house, hiding in the shadows of the woods to avoid detection. Could he find a way to sneak in and get warm? That was when he noticed another peculiar thing.

On this side of the house, there were no windows!

"What is this place?" he whispered to himself.

Continuing his search, he finally came across a small, barred opening. These bars were definitely made to keep everyone out, including children. *What on earth could this be?* he wondered.

CHAPTER THREE
Help!

PEERING INTO the opening, Basil hoped to find some kind of friendly shelter. A shaft of daylight was all that pierced the darkness of the room behind the bars.

This opening was actually at the top of the dark room, and in the dim shadows he could make out a barren floor far below.

What was that down there?

Something moved in the darkness. Not something. Someone! It was Louise!

"LOUISE!" Basil whispered as loud as he dared.

Her head snapped up, and she looked at him in surprise as he struggled in vain to squeeze through the bars.

Quickly, Louise put her finger to her lips. "Shhhh," she whispered. "You need to be silent." Then she pointed at the cell door. She was being watched!

How did Louise get there? Why was she being held captive? And who would kidnap her? But for now, the answers didn't matter—Basil just had to find a way to get her out. "Hold on," he whispered. "I'll be back!"

Searching the grounds for a way to sneak in, Basil came to see that this foreboding place was more a fortress than a home. And the industrial smokestacks told him that something big must be going on inside.

Coming around a corner, Basil spotted a small opening that didn't have bars or locks. Like the iron fence, it was too small an opening for a grown man to get through, but it was big enough for a boy his age.

Upon closer inspection, Basil saw that it was just an ordinary coal chute. *Perfect.* He had no idea where it led, but he quickly crawled inside.

The combination of his sopping wet clothing and thick coal dust made the metal walls of the chute very slick. *Zoom!* Basil's slide down the pitch-black tunnel was a lot faster than he wanted, but he managed to keep himself from screaming . . . even though he really wanted to! His frightening slide ended with a muffled thud, and Basil found himself in an enormous coal bin—far larger than any he had ever seen. Peering out, he could see rail tracks that must have been used to haul the coal.

Following the tracks, he could see the glow of a roaring fire. But it was more than just a fire; it was a blast furnace.

Basil was covered from head to toe in coal soot. As filthy and sneezy as he felt, it was great to be able to hide in shadows, and the roar of the blast furnace muffled the sound of his footsteps. *Tiptoe, tiptoe.* He moved about the immense, underground labyrinth undetected.

Doorways were everywhere. Stairs led up to more
doors, and hallways connected to even more hallways.
A tangled system of pipes and heavy beams supported
pulleys linked with heavy chains. *Something important
is going on here,* Basil reasoned, *and when something
important is being done with this amount of secrecy, it can't
be anything good.*

So far, dumb luck had been on Basil's side, but he
knew he couldn't depend on that. He needed a plan.
But I'm just an ordinary boy, he thought. *What do I know
about such things? How can I make a plan when I don't
even know where I am?*

Just as things seemed to be doomed to failure, an oddly tall man appeared from one of the hallways and headed up a stairway to a door. The man's slow, purposeful gait made Basil think he might be someone of importance. *What do I have to lose by following him?* Basil wondered, hoping the man might lead him to the cell holding Louise.

Basil kept himself hidden in the shadows of the dungeon-like corridor as he followed the tall man. Echoing through the hallways was a constant *boom-boom-boom*, the methodical noise of machinery. *BOOM-BOOM!* The sound became louder and louder as Basil kept pace, trying not to lose sight of the important-looking man. Soon the noise was almost deafening, and it seemed to be coming from a hallway the man passed before disappearing through another door.

What could be making so much noise? Is this a factory?
Basil wondered. He peeked around the corner of the
hallway, making sure no one was there to see him. He
stopped in his tracks. "What on earth . . . ?" The roar of
chains and grinding gears overpowered the sound of
his voice.

"What IS this place?" he whispered aloud. The
answer to that innocent question would soon have an
effect on the whole world.

The hallway entrance had led him to a huge, multi-level room. It was indeed a factory, but nothing could have prepared him for this. The complex assembly line and machinery were far beyond the technology of Basil's time. And as he listened to the *BOOM-BOOM-*

BOOM of the heavy metal chains and machines, he thought he could detect some strange kind of musical theme in it all. But it wasn't music. It was like the opposite of music. It made Basil feel sick inside.

What are they making? he wondered. Whatever it was, it was fearful, not friendly. The metal objects passing him on hooks looked like life-sized dolls of some sort, only made of metal. And Basil could guess from the look of them that these weren't toys.

On the level below, carried on a conveyor belt, were the bottom half of these machines. *Is that how they move around?* Basil wondered. *Are they big mechanical dolls of some sort?*

Suddenly a horn blasted—the loudest horn Basil had ever heard. Having lived in a lighthouse, he had heard some pretty loud horns on ships passing by in the fog. But this one beat them all, and Basil had to hold his hands over his ears to quiet the painful sound. Mercifully, it finally stopped. *Must be a break time for the workers,* Basil reasoned. He was right. And when the workers left, Basil took his chance and went down to get a closer look. *What was going on?* He still hid in the shadows as much as possible in case someone returned.

Looking closer at the machines didn't reveal what they were or what they could do, but the whole place gave Basil a frightening feeling. At first he thought the arms of these mechanical men were simply pipes. But then it struck him that they weren't pipes. They were more like small cannon barrels!

Voices began to echo down a hallway, and the sound of gears started to fill the room. Basil panicked.

He needed to find a hiding place or escape quickly. *I'm going to get caught!* His only choice was a door on the second level.

He ran as fast as he could, hoping it was unlocked and that no one was on the other side. His hands were still coated with coal dust, making it hard to get a grip on the doorknob. In minutes the workers would come back, and Basil was in plain sight.

Desperate, he tried to use his coat sleeve to get a better grip, but the doorknob was just as slick as his hands.

Oh no! The knob began to turn on its own! Someone was coming from the other side. *There is nowhere to hide! The door is at the end of the room, and if I run the other way, I'll run into the returning workers!*

As the door swung open, Basil flattened himself against the wall as tightly as he could. Instinctively, he shut his eyes, as if that would make him invisible. *Footsteps. Shuffling papers.* Then something brushed across his face.

When Basil dared to open his eyes, the tall man was walking past him, his long white lab coat flowing behind like a cape. He was deep in thought as he read the papers he was shuffling. He never noticed the frail little boy hugging the wall.

Quick as a wink, Basil slipped inside the door before it closed on its own. *Click.* The door locked.

He found himself inside an opulent room that gave the impression of great wealth. This, he decided, must be the private office of the tall man. Everything was built to the scale of a person of great height. That made it difficult for a boy of such an ordinary size to see what was on the desk.

The walls, from the floors to the high ceilings, were covered with blueprints and other technical drawings of intricate machines and parts. They were far too complicated for Basil to even begin to grasp.

Climbing up on the large, plush chair, Basil searched the top of the huge desk, trying to find some clues about what was going on in this factory. The desktop was very neat and orderly. No loose papers, just a large book off on one end.

Basil took a look. On the cover, the title read, *The Manifesto for World Peace Through Domination.*

Although Basil's mother always told him that you couldn't judge a book by its cover, Basil thought this might be the exception. It wasn't a fun adventure story to read at the beach. As he skimmed through the pages of detailed notes about the factory, Basil realized his suspicions were right. No toys were being made here. These were weapons! And not just ordinary firearms, but mechanical soldiers . . . indestructible soldiers! Someone was building an army!

But why?

As he read further, Basil discovered the diabolical plans of a madman. The book was obviously written by a genius, but a madman nonetheless. Basil remembered the sense of dread he felt when he first saw the tall, ominous-looking man. Now he knew his instincts were correct.

This man wants to rule the world, Basil thought, *and he's set up an intricate network of spies throughout Europe. They're all waiting for one event to set the plan in motion. It's a plan that has been in the works for years, maybe even decades. And it's almost ready to be unleashed.*

Basil read on. The tall man intended to create a problem that would make countries go to war with one another. Soon the entire world would be engulfed in armed conflict . . . a world war. It would be warfare on a scale never imagined before. Such a massive war would destroy the armies of the mightiest nations. That's when the tall man's secret mechanical army would be set into motion. They would be able to defeat every army from every country in one great sweep.

This massive destruction, it was reasoned, would finally bring about world peace. The plan was as flawless as it was frightening. But it was all delicately balanced on just one event. Without this one event, their entire plan would fall apart.

Then Basil suddenly understood the missing piece. The event they needed was happening right now. They needed to launch their attack from Helios to make it work. But first they had to *find* the great city floating in the clouds. Then they needed a way to get up to it and take over the city.

"Louise . . ." he whispered. It all began to make sense. Now he understood why they attacked the flying pteranodon and captured the girl. Beatrice's flight had unwittingly provided this madman with the opportunity he had been patiently waiting for—a way to locate Helios.

There was no time left. Basil had to find Louise quickly. Then somehow they had to get back to warn the people of Helios. . . .

Running out through another door, Basil stopped and peeked down a dark hallway.

Someone was turning a corner down another, long corridor. *He's got something in his hands,* Basil thought. *It looks like a bowl of food and a cup of water.* Not knowing what else to do, Basil decided to follow him. The squat, hunchbacked man went down a flight of stairs, then another, then another. Finally he came to a heavy wooden door. The man bent down to open a hatch at the bottom of the door. He slid the bowl and cup in. Then he left.

Waiting until the man was out of sight, Basil rushed to the door. It was locked. He opened the hatch at the bottom. Peering through, he saw darkness—and one small shaft of sunlight. That was all the light he needed. He saw Louise!

Basil squeezed through the small hatch, and the two celebrated. But they had no way of knowing this would actually be the easiest part of their adventure.

In a whisper, Basil told Louise about the insidious plot. He fully expected that she wouldn't believe such a horrible tale. Instead, she surprised him. Her entire body slumped in sadness. Her head slowly bowed, and she cupped her face in her hands.

"It must be him," she said softly. Then she exclaimed, "I thought he was just a myth!"

"Who?"

"Von Röttweil," she said in a hushed tone. "Dr. Euric Von Röttweil . . ."

"So who is he? Where does he come from?" Basil asked, still trying to understand.

"Well," Louise said with a frown, "supposedly, he was once the most respected member of the High Council of Helios. He was brilliant. Everyone thought he would rise to be Council Leader some day. He was known for his speeches about world peace."

"But world peace is a good thing, right?" Basil asked.

"He made everyone *think* he was a man of peace," she continued, "and he was almost given complete control of Helios. But then someone exposed Von Röttweil's real intentions. His idea of peace was to conquer the world and rule over it through fear! He wanted to use the superior technology of Helios to keep the rest of the world under his power. He called it 'peace through domination.'"

"So what happened to him?"

"My mother used to tell us the story when we were little. At the end, Von Röttweil was banished from Helios. What a horrible thing. They took away all of his Helios technology and made it impossible for him to even know how to find Helios. That was the part of the story that made my little sister hide under the bed."

"How could he not find Helios if he came from there?" Basil asked.

"There are secrets," Louise said solemnly. "Secrets only a few people know. My mother knows them. And other things . . ." She paused, then went on. "As the story goes, Von Röttweil swore vengeance and would one day return to carry out his evil plan. But that was so long ago, long before I was even born. We all thought it was just a scary fable."

"It must not be just a fable," Basil said, "and he's not a myth. I've seen him."

"Wait," Louise blurted out, suddenly optimistic. "He needs an airship to get back to Helios! If he had one, he would have gone there already!"

"Well . . ." Basil said haltingly, "that's why you're so important to him. You're the key to the success of his entire plan."

The look on her face told Basil he didn't need to explain any further. She could see the whole plot.

"I'm . . . I'm the bait," she whispered. Then, gathering herself, she said quietly yet urgently, "We've got to get out of here before a rescue party flies down!"

"I know!" Basil shot back. "But how are we going to set you free?"

Once again Louise said something he never could have expected. "We need to break this chain. Get the flute from my bag!"

Sure enough, in the corner of the cell was a satchel. As instructed, Basil reached in and found a flute carved from a bamboo stalk. At first, he just stared at it. "How in the world is a flute going to break that metal chain?"

"It's a trick Professor McGookin taught us back in kindergarten," Louise told him as she snatched the flute from his hands. "Professor McGookin isn't only a music teacher. He's a scientist who studies the effects of sound and sound waves. A lot of what makes Helios the way it is has to do with ninth-dimensional

music. You people on the ground do know about the
ninth dimension, don't you?"

Basil just shook his head no.

"Well, if I can find the right pitch and hold it long
enough, it will make the tumblers in the lock vibrate
and open up," she went on. "It's really very simple.
Any five-year-old can do it."

She raised the flute to her lips and gently began to
play. Her tiny fingers gingerly moved over the holes,
trying to find the right key. Basil was expecting to
hear a tune, but he only heard a string of unrelated
tones. In fact, his ears were starting to hurt.

"How long is this going to take?" Basil asked, cupping his ears.

"You'll know I'm getting close when I hit the sound you can't hear," Louise said patiently.

Gradually, the sounds became softer, easing the pain in Basil's ears. Then he didn't hear anything—but Louise was still playing the flute.

At first this frightened him. Had he gone deaf? But then he heard another sound. It was just barely audible, but it was a wonderful sound! A simple *click* came from the lock holding Louise to the thick, heavy chain. Could the flute have actually worked? Basil reached for the lock and pulled.

It didn't open, but Basil felt it move. So he pulled on it again . . . and again. It still wouldn't open. He whacked at it and walked away in frustration.

Clunk.

The lock snapped open and fell to the hard stone floor. Louise was free!

Both of them scampered up the steps to the door.

Slowly, Basil opened the hatch, just a crack. He peeked out. Was anyone here?

It was quiet, and the hallway was empty. He crawled out first and then pulled Louise through. They were lost in a labyrinth of halls and stairways, each ending with a door. The wrong door would lead them right back into the clutches of their captors. Could they find the right door?

CHAPTER FOUR
More Surprises

SUDDENLY IT hit Basil. "Listen for the machinery," he whispered. "When it's loud, we need to go the other way. The people are operating the machines!"

They crept away from the sounds of the factory, putting their ears to any door before opening it.

"That must be his sound," Louise whispered. "Von Röttweil's sound. It's so heavy. Like hatred. We don't have sounds like that in Helios."

Each time they came to a door, they opened it just enough to peek through the crack. It was a slow process, and they were running out of time.

When they pushed open the fifth door, bright light burst through. *Yes!* At the end of a long hallway was an open door, leading outside to daylight!

"Quick!" Louise whispered. "We have to find Beatrice. We've got to get back to Helios! If anyone comes looking for us, they'll be ambushed by these maniacs!"

With that, they ran down the hall and out into the woods. Right away, Basil recognized the path leading back to the bay. "Let's head in that direction. Maybe Beatrice is hidden down there!"

As the two disappeared into the thick trees high above them, a dim, yellow light glowed from a window in the ominous house. A tall, shadowy figure stood motionless, looking down.

Behind him, a trapdoor opened. "Za prisoner has escaped, Herr Doctor," the oafish henchman growled.

"Ya," Dr. Von Röttweil replied softly, "just as I knew zey vould. She's a very smart little girl."

"But if zey keep going zat vay," the puggish man grunted, "zey vill find za flying creature!"

"Ya," Von Röttweil calmly replied. "Make sure zat zey do. Everyzing depends on it."

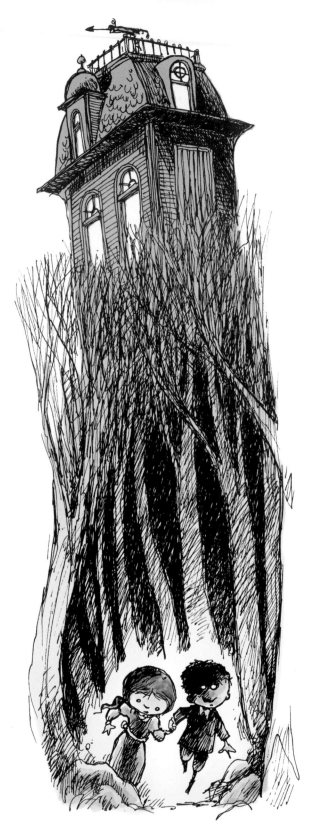

Meanwhile, Basil and Louise ran frantically. Where were they headed? And what would happen if Von Röttweil discovered that Louise had escaped? They had to get as far away from that horrid place as they could.

"We've got to find Beatrice!" Louise cried, her voice quivering. She feared the worst. Who knew what Von Röttweil might have done to her beloved pteranodon?

Suddenly Basil stopped in his tracks. There, in a clearing just ahead, was Beatrice! She had been tethered to keep her quiet and grounded. "They've tied her beak!" cried Louise. "A pteranodon's screech can be heard for miles. We've got to untie her but try to keep her quiet!"

Basil watched with fascination as Louise untied her loyal friend. "Wow," Basil said excitedly, "what a stroke of luck!" Then, pondering his ordinary life, he realized something extraordinary.

"I've never been this lucky before!"

His happiness was interrupted by an ear-piercing screech. "Shhhh, Bea! You have to be quiet! They'll find us!" Louise said, untangling the rope. But when Beatrice spread her aching wings and stretched her legs, she continued her long, angry scream.

A strange thought crossed Basil's mind—a thought that erased the broad smile on his face. Could it be that luck had nothing to do with finding Beatrice so quickly?

Louise tried her best to calm her giant pet as Beatrice's high-pitched screech reached up into the atmosphere, carrying for miles. Surely Von Röttweil and his people could hear it.

"Hurry, Louise!" Basil cried.

But it wasn't just Von Röttweil who could hear it.

Hovering high above the clouds in the great airship, a familiar figure heard it, too. "Ah, there they are!" The rotund figure peering over the stern was none other than Professor McGookin. Following the familiar screech, he dropped the airship below the protective clouds in search of the lost children. Louise was forbidden to leave Helios, but no doubt she and Basil had been having so much fun they'd lost track of time and had wandered off.

From his tower, Von Röttweil continued to watch the skies through his powerful telescope. Spotting a large object floating down from the clouds, he brought it into focus. His eyes lit up with evil delight. "McGookin!" he exclaimed. "Ve meet again, old friend. . . ."

Then turning to his assistant, he spoke in a calm but vicious tone. "Release za drones!"

His brutish assistant quickly reached for a large lever nearby and began to pull. The grinding sound of heavy chains and gears rumbled from below. Slowly a large metal door began to slide open. The methodical sound of machinery starting up inside grew louder and louder.

Meanwhile, as the professor slowly descended, he tried to follow the sound of Beatrice's angry wail. Louise was successful in calming her pet, so McGookin pulled out his powerful telescope, hoping to spot the children before the sun set.

Looking straight down at the ground, he saw nothing but trees. He slowly scanned from side to side, then up, as they might have already taken flight.

Grrummmm . . . Boom . . . Grrummmm . . . Another noise filled the air. It was low and threatening, with a dark sound. Not music, but like a nasty thunderstorm approaching from the distance.

At first, swinging his telescope in the direction of the sound, the professor again saw only trees. Then something flashed, reflecting the sunlight.

More flashes appeared, faster and faster. Was it something to do with the children? The professor lowered his ship and steered toward the flashing lights. When he lifted his telescope again, he could make out a house . . . a very large house with a tower. He glided in closer for a better look.

Focusing on the tower, the professor spotted someone standing in the window—a shadowy figure with a familiar look.

No, it can't be. The professor's jovial manner vanished. His eyes narrowed into a deadly serious squint.

"Von Röttweil . . ." he murmured.

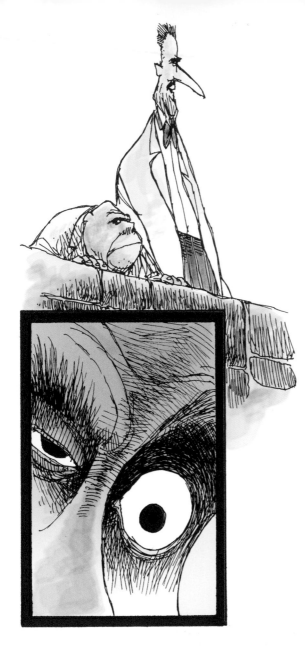

Von Röttweil walked out to the balcony of the tower. He had the cold confidence of someone who had carefully calculated every move. A wry smile exposed the meticulously white teeth of a perfectionist. "Ah," he said with pure hatred. "So it's za professor who has come! Zis is even better zan vatt I had planned! Prepare to fire za minipoons!" he ordered. Then, turning a poisonous glare at the vulnerable airship gliding closer, he cast the final blow.

"Time for retribution, my old friend," Von Röttweil hissed.

By now, the airship was close enough for Professor McGookin to see what was reflecting the sunlight on the ground below. Surrounding the gigantic house were hundreds of mechanical soldiers. *Clank. Clank.* More poured out of the huge factory doors.

Click! In unison, the heads of the soldiers turned up. Every eye sensor pointed directly at the airship. *Chicka . . . Chicka . . .* Their arms began to lift. Each robot rested on a platform that rotated in any direction, built like modern-day tanks. Each soldier's arm was actually a cannon, and every cannon was loaded with a miniature harpoon—"minipoons."

The momentum of the airship was bringing it closer and lower. The professor, seeing the cannons rising, turned the wheel hard. Quickly, he began to throw everything he could overboard. If he made the ship lighter, it would rise faster.

The great ship creaked and groaned. The propellers spun faster and faster. Moments later, another sound filled the air: *foomp*. Then: *foomp-foomp-foomp*.

The professor didn't need to look. He knew what it was. With all his might, he continued to turn the wheel.

Soon he heard a whistling sound. It wasn't the sound he most feared. In fact, the whistling brought a little smile to his face as he watched several minipoons sail under the bow of the ship. But his smile disappeared quickly. This was only the first round of minipoon shots. It wouldn't be long before the mechanical soldiers got their bearings. They'd be adjusting their sites, so he had to keep the ship moving.

"Fire za next volley," Von Röttweil ordered, "but keep za aim low. I don't vant za balloon punctured!"

As the ship made another hard turn, more robots were poised and ready: *foomp-foomp-foomp-foomp-foomp-foomp-foomp-foomp-foomp-foomp-foomp-foomp!*

The first few minipoons still whistled past, just below the hull. Then the professor heard the sickening sound he had been dreading . . . *THUNK!*

Then another . . . *THUNK!* . . . and another and

another and another. *THUNK-THUNK-THUNK-THUNK-THUNK!* Minipoons were striking the hull. The ropes attached to them tightened up, stopping the ship's movement. The professor couldn't pull away.

Grabbing a hatchet, McGookin leaned over the rail.

He held on to one of the ropes holding the balloon as he swung at the minipoons. Could he break them before the ship was reeled in? He chopped off the first two with ease. The third was barely within reach, and he took a few swipes before breaking that one off as well.

Now the strain of the ship was on his side as the ropes on the last two minpoons began to stretch. *Pop!* One of them snapped.

The ship suddenly lurched. Professor McGookin almost lost his grip. He had to get back in the ship, and this was quite an effort for a man of his size. The last rope was straining. Would it break? He had to be ready to maneuver again.

THUNK! THUNK! The awful sound of minipoons striking the hull was back. Once more, the professor grabbed the hatchet. He looked over the bow. No minipoons. Over the stern. No minipoons. He leaned over farther. Minipoons had struck directly below, on the very bottom of the hull. They were completely out of the professor's reach.

"Ahhh . . ." Von Röttweil purred, congratulating himself. "Just as planned. Ze airship is as good as mine!"

His henchman began to turn a huge wheel, and the minipoon ropes tightened. Slowly the airship was being reeled to Earth by the robots—carefully so they didn't break the ropes or rip the hooks out of the hull. Von Röttweil was in no hurry. He had been waiting for this prize for years.

Just then, a shadow passed over the evil doctor. It was followed by something he wasn't expecting . . . an ear-piecing screech. It could only mean one thing: the huge wings of Beatrice were soaring overhead.

With mighty downstrokes, the pteranodon streaked higher and higher, into the protective cloak of clouds above the airship.

"Don't fire!" Von Röttweil ordered. "Ze minipoons might hit ze balloon! I need zat airship!"

Riding on the back of the great flying reptile, Louise and Basil held on tightly. Beatrice spread her wings wide, silently riding a thermal updraft while Louise waited for the right moment.

"Now, Bea!" Louise shouted. "Dive!"

Beatrice folded her giant wings in and stretched her head down. *Zoom!* They plummeted at rocket speed. The sound of air whooshing past them was almost deafening. Louise had to shout as loud as she could for Beatrice to hear her. "Swoop, Bea! Swoop!"

With that, Beatrice approached the airship. She
spread her wings again as she headed toward the
professor's boat. Then she opened her great beak. It
was lined with razor-sharp teeth.

Beatrice swooped under the airship at lightning
speed, catching all the lines in her beak. *Snap!* She easily
sliced all of them as she swooped back up to the clouds.

As the taut ropes suddenly broke, the airship jolted
upward.

Von Röttweil's eyes narrowed in fury. He had lost the element of surprise. Now he watched his prize escaping. "Reload and fire!" he shouted. "Don't let him get avay!"

"Vot about za children, Herr Doctor?" the henchman asked.

"Zere is no shortage of children in za vorld," Von Röttweil snarled. "Zey are expendable. Shoot zem down."

Once the airship was free, the professor regained his composure.

Like a chess master who has been paralyzed by an unforeseen move, he took a deep breath and calmly assessed the situation. What should his next move be? He would not allow anger to cloud his judgment.

"You had your shot, Von Röttweil," he shouted down through gritted teeth. "But you'll not get another!"

Then, forcing a smile, the
professor began to hum—quietly at first,
then louder. It was the same mysterious tune that
Basil had whistled from his window in the lighthouse.

Turning the wheel once again, the professor pulled several levers and flipped a panel of switches. He chose a bold move in return. Rather than steer away from the conflict, the ship creaked and groaned under the strain of bringing it into a steep descent.

"H-H-Herr Doctor," the henchman stammered as stark surprise turned to fear. "He's heading directly toward us!"

Von Röttweil cast his emotionless, steely glare at the rapidly approaching airship. "Vot are you up to, McGookin?"

Meanwhile, high above the action, Basil turned to look back. "Louise!" Basil cried out in alarm. "He . . . he's steering the ship right at them!"

Knowing the professor as well as she did, Louise tried to lessen Basil's fears—and her own. "He knows what he's doing . . . I hope."

"Vot iz ze professor's plan?" The airship was approaching too fast now for the robots to track it and make an accurate shot.

The professor knew that Von Röttweil had only one option. The professor planned to use it to his advantage, but he had to time his move precisely.

"Ve must bring down ze airship without ruining it. Ze professor cannot get avay! He vill bring back ze forces of Helios. Fire at vill!" he shouted down to his army.

With that, the robots filled the air with minipoons. Von Röttweil hoped that some would hit.

By now, the airship was at treetop level. Just as the minipoons fired, the professor shot a mooring hook at a tall, thick fir tree. As the hook wrapped around the tree, the professor quickly secured the line, forcing the ship to take a sharp turn and spin around the tree. As it spun, minipoon after minipoon sailed past harmlessly.

"Vot iz he doing?" Von Röttweil said aloud. He hesitated for a moment. "Vot iz his plan?"

Whoosh! The ship spun full circle around the tree,

picking up even more speed. The sweet sound of music began to fill the air.

Sweat broke out on Von Röttweil's face. "Reload! Ve must bring down zat . . ." In midsentence the horrible doctor stopped. A trapdoor had sprung open under the bow of the ship.

He instantly understood that his moment of hesitation was all the time the professor had needed.

Von Röttweil's commanding presence waned as his eyes widened in terror. "Oh, no," he whispered, "not za thermablat!"

A grim smile spread across Louise's face. She turned to Basil and sharply ordered, "Hold on tight! The shockwave is going to . . ."

But before she could finish, the great airship blasted up past them, traveling backward faster than Basil could blink. Feeling an invisible force heaving them up from below, Basil held on as they began to follow the airship's path—higher and higher.

After two minutes, Louise allowed Beatrice to slow down and glide on her own.

Looking below from the safety
of the pteranodon's wings, all
Basil and Louise could see
was a billowing cloud of
smoke and dust. The
black haze obscured
everything on
the ground for
miles around.

"What on earth
just happened?" Basil asked.
"Hopefully," Louise replied gently,
"the end of Von Röttweil's plans."

Just as quickly as it had started, the battle was over.
An eerie silence replaced the frantic din of warfare.

Professor McGookin signaled Louise to bring
Beatrice closer to the airship. With a gentle tug of the
reins, Louise steered her mighty pet to slowly glide to
the port side of the ship, matching its speed.

"Basil," the professor called in his soothing baritone.
"Come, dear boy. It's long past time to get you home."

Basil looked down at the destruction below. Clouds
of dust were settling. What was a formidable armament

factory just minutes ago had been laid waste, along with Von Röttweil's plans to rule the world with his mechanized army. The devastation appeared to be complete.

"What was that, Professor?" Basil asked, still not quite believing what he had witnessed.

"It's called a thermablat. It's a weapon I invented that operates on sound waves rather than explosives. And I'm afraid that's all I can tell you about it, except that this is just a small one. The big ones are part of the defense system of Helios. The less you know about this, the safer you and the rest of civilization will be."

"But I don't understand, Professor. How did you make that happen?"

"Oh, I suppose it's safe enough to tell you one little thing. Let's just say it's all in the music, dear boy," he said with a huge grin. "It's the music of the spheres. It's the harmony and joy that emanate from magnetic fields of notes in the ninth dimension. They move every time you smile—and in your case, whistle a tune. It's the reason music makes you feel so good. Magic, isn't it? Today it's one of our secrets, Laddie. But some day . . ."

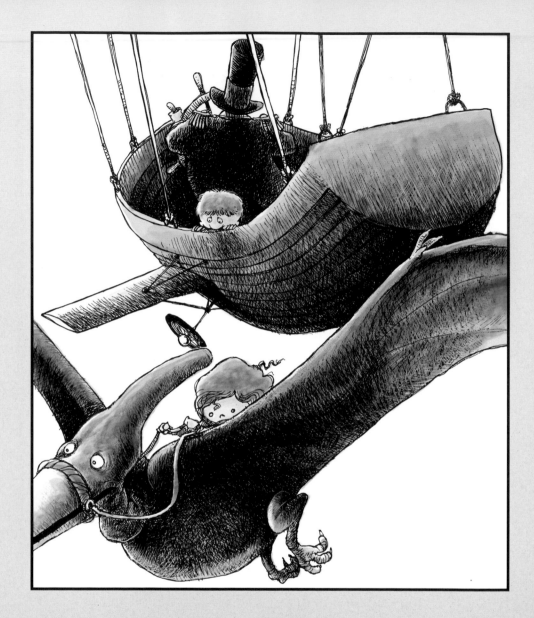

The professor turned his attention to Louise. "And you, my mischievous young lady, need to get back to Helios!"

"Yes, sir," she said unhappily, but she perked up when a new idea crossed her agile mind.

"Can we take Basil to see Monkey Island? It's on the way back!"

The professor sighed. "Where is that boy, anyway?"

For a split second they were frightened. Had they lost him? But then they spotted Basil. He was curled up in a spool of rope and had fallen fast asleep.

"I think he's had enough for now, Louise," the professor said kindly. "Maybe some other time. Now you and Beatrice get home. Your parents are probably worried to death. Your mother and the other High Council leaders will want to know every detail."

"But Professor, can I ask you one last question?"

"Go ahead, Louise."

"How did you find him? Basil, I mean. How did you know?"

"Aha!" said McGookin, laughing aloud. "He's one of us! I could hear it in his voice, Louise. The notes, you know. His kind come along every century or so. They don't come when you go looking for them, but they always come on time. Like today, eh? And you need to be off now!"

"OK, OK," Louise said. Then, with just a gentle tug on the reins, she called out, "Home, Bea!" With that, the mighty pteranodon flapped her powerful wings and headed off. Beatrice's homing instincts unerringly sent her toward Helios.

As the great airship drifted silently away, a lone, tall figure stood amid the ruins below.

He watched as they faded into the horizon.

"Curse you, McGookin," he grumbled. "I vill haf my revenge!"

CHAPTER FIVE
Snowing Again

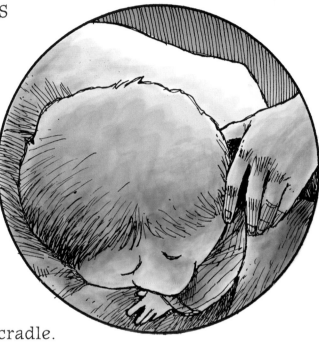

THE SUN WAS setting, and the gentle rocking of the airship soothed Basil in his deep sleep. Rocking, rocking . . . just like when he was a baby in his cradle.

The rocking grew a little more jolting, and Basil was nudged from his slumber. He heard a familiar voice.

"Time to get up, sleepyhead," he heard the voice say—a voice that sounded just like his mother. "You've got a lot of chores to do that you were supposed to do yesterday, young man."

Sitting bolt upright, Basil found himself back in his bed. He looked over at the window. It was snowing outside. Again. As usual.

"M . . . M . . .
Mommy?" he
sputtered. "How . . .
what . . . ?" Basil's
mind was spinning
too fast to form
an intelligent
thought.

"My, my," his
mother said in a
loving voice. "You must have had quite a day playing
yesterday."

Basil's eyes widened. What did his mother say? "A
day?" he gasped. "All that happened in just a day?"

"All what, dear?" his mother asked in that half-
interested manner grown-ups have when they're not
really listening to you.

But Basil pressed on, breathlessly. "I met a
professor, and I traveled in his flying ship . . . to
Helios, a sparkling city floating on the clouds . . . and
there was Louise, and her giant pet reptile that flies . . .
and Dr. Von Röttweil captured Louise. . . . I saved her!

I rescued her from his dungeon! It was below a factory where he was making an army of mechanical soldiers! And the professor saved the world from tyrannical rule by this madman with just one blast from a sound weapon called a thermablat . . . and there was music—music from another dimension. . . ."

But his mother kept folding his laundry and putting it away in his dresser. "Goodness," she said once Basil finally paused to take a breath. "That sounds like quite an exciting dream!"

Basil stopped cold. He slumped down into the pillows. "A dream?" he moaned. "Is that all it was? A dream?"

His mother finished putting away his clothing and headed out the door. "Oh," she said, stopping in the doorway. "I almost forgot. A little girl came by early this morning and asked if you could go to Monkey Island with her. She's very nice. I don't recall seeing her before. Do you know what she was talking about?"

"No," Basil replied with a broad grin. "But I can't *wait* to find out."

Internationally respected cartoonist

WILEY MILLER

created his daily comic strip "Non Sequitur" in 1992.
In its first year of publication, it was named Best Newspaper
Comic Strip of the Year by the National Cartoonists Society
and is currently published in more than 800 newspapers in
20 countries. In 2005, Wiley Miller pointed his pen in a new
direction: a comic strip with a story designed to be expanded
into a children's book for the Blue Sky Press. "Ordinary Basil"
was introduced to the world as a full-color, Sunday strip, and
Miller was deluged with letters from delighted children
and their parents. Known for his humor, wit, and an uncanny
ability to capture character, Wiley Miller is an artist who loved
adventure stories as a child and has now created his own. Miller
lives in Maine with his wife. This is his first book for children.